CLOCK SHOP

MR. WINKY
WATCHES · CLOCKS

SAME DAY SERVICE

STORY BY JEAN HORTON BERG ★ PICTURES BY ART SEIDEN

G+D VINTAGE

r. Winky mended clocks. He took care of shabby clocks with dirty faces, poor old clocks with broken hands, and lazy clocks that wouldn't run.

After he fixed a clock, Mr. Winky wound it. Then he put it back on the shelf to wait for its owner to come and take it home.

Mr. Winky's clock shop was a cheerful place.
The clocks on the shelves kept up a constant chatter.
TICKETY-TICK, said the little ones.

TOCK-TOCK, said the big ones. The Swiss clock sang
a tinkly little song. The cuckoo popped out of the
cuckoo clock and said, CUCKOO, CUCKOO, CUCKOO.
(The grandfather clock tried to chime first, but
the cuckoo clock always beat him!)

One day Mr. Winky was sitting at his workbench, enjoying all the TICKS and **TOCKS**, and TING-A-LINGS, and **DINGS** and **DONGS**, and CUCKOOS, and BONG-BONGS, when the door of the shop flew open.

"Hello, Mr. Glum," said Mr. Winky. "What can I do for you?"

"Oh my," said Mr. Glum, sticking his fingers in his ears, "how can you stand this awful noise? I was going to visit with you awhile, but I can't hear myself think! Good-bye, Mr. Winky! GOOD-BYE!"

Mr. Glum pulled his hat down over his ears and hurried out, slamming the door behind him.

At first Mr. Winky laughed. Then he felt hurt. "He could have been a little more polite," he murmured. Then he tried to think of something clever to say to Mr. Glum next time he saw him. He tried and tried, but he couldn't think of a single thing.

"Why," he cried, sticking his fingers in his ears, "this place is so noisy I can't hear *myself* think!" He jumped up from his workbench, pulled his hat down on his head, and hurried out, slamming the door behind him.

"It's nice and quiet out here," he said as he walked briskly down the street. He looked to the right and to the left, and was just about to step off the curb when SQUOONK—a taxi horn blew, and SQUEEECH—some brakes squealed. Mr. Winky jumped a foot into the air as the taxi whizzed by.

"Whew! That was a narrow squeak," he said. He looked up and down the street again, and then stepped off the curb. CLANG-CLANG-CLANG, screeched a trolley car.

"Oohh!" howled Mr. Winky. He pulled his hat down on his head and ran as fast as he could to the railroad station. "I must get out of the city," he said. "It's so noisy I can't hear myself think!"

He bought a ticket to the country. As the train rushed through the countryside, he settled in the red plush seat and opened a bag of peanuts. SNAP-CRACKLE-CRUNCH-CRUNCH-CRUNCH-CRUNCH—Mr. Winky ate peanuts.

WHO-OOOO-OOOO—the train whistled. PICKETY-PICK, POCKETY-POCK, PICKETY-PICK, POCKETY-POCK—the wheels clattered over the rails. CLICK-CLICK, CLICK-CLICK— the conductor punched tickets.

"Oh my," said Mr. Winky, sticking his fingers in his ears, "I can't stand this noise. I can't hear myself think!"

He put the rest of the peanuts in his pocket and got off the train at the next stop.

As Mr. Winky walked slowly down a dusty country lane, he saw a little red farmhouse.

"Come in, come in," said the farmer. "You're just in time for dinner."

Mr. Winky went out to the pump to wash his hands.

SQUEEK, SQUEEK—the pump handle hopped up and down, and the cold water splashed into the bucket. Mr. Winky washed his hands and went into the house.

Dinner was delicious. Mr. Winky's plate was piled high with rosy ham, mashed potatoes, green peas, and applesauce.

But the jangling of the knives and forks and the clattering of the dishes were too much for him.

"I can't stand this noise," he said, sticking his fingers in his ears. "Oh my, I can't hear myself think!"

He finished his dinner quickly, thanked the farmer, and hurried upstairs to bed.

"I'll take a walk in the wild woods," he said the next morning. "Surely it will be quiet there!"

Mr. Winky walked farther and farther into the wild woods. It was very quiet.

"Ah," said Mr. Winky. "This is more like it. At last I can hear myself think!" He set his hat on top of his head and walked briskly through the trees.

CHEEEE! clattered a red squirrel.

Mr. Winky walked a little faster.

CAAWWW! screamed a raggedy black crow,

swooping down through the shadows.

Mr. Winky began to run.

Leaves crackled and branches snapped as he ran. "Ouch!" howled Mr. Winky when he bumped into a tree. "Ow!" howled Mr. Winky when he tripped over an old stump. And "Oh my!" gasped Mr. Winky when he ran smack into a big brown bear.

GRRRR! roared the big brown bear, sitting up on its hind legs.

Mr. Winky turned right-about-face, and ran.

GRRRR! said the bear.

CAW! said the crow.

CHEE! said the red squirrel.

"I can't stand this noise," muttered Mr. Winky, and sticking his fingers in his ears, he hurried out of the wild woods.

He hurried past the little red farmhouse, and past the pump, and down to the railroad station. There he bought a ticket back to the city.

As the train rushed through the countryside, he settled back in the red plush seat and began to eat peanuts. SNAP-CRACKLE-CRUNCH-CRUNCH-CRUNCH-CRUNCH—Mr. Winky ate some peanuts.

WHO-0000-0000— the train whistled. PICKETY-PICK, POCKETY-POCK, PICKETY-PICK, POCKETY-POCK— the wheels clattered over the rails, and CLICK-CLICK, CLICK-CLICK —the conductor punched tickets.

Mr. Winky got off the train when it reached the city, and started toward his clock shop.

CLANG-CLANG-CLANG, screeched a trolley car.

EEEE-EEEE-EEEE, shrieked the siren on a big fire engine.

SQUONK-SQUONK-SQUONKETY-SQUONK, tooted a taxi horn.

Mr. Winky watched for his chance, then scuttled across the street and hurried into his shop.

He didn't wait to take his hat off before he went over to his workbench.

But something was wrong. What was the matter? Mr. Winky looked around uneasily. He looked at his workbench. All his tools were in place.

He opened the drawer where he kept his money. All his money was there.

He looked for his glasses. They were right where they belonged, on his face.

WHAT COULD BE WRONG?

"Oh my!" said Mr. Winky. "It's *quiet* in here.
There isn't a sound!" And sure enough, there wasn't
a single TICK or **TOCK** to be heard. The clocks hadn't
been wound, and they all had stopped!

"I can't stand this silence!" roared Mr. Winky, sticking his fingers in his ears. He went right to work and began winding the clocks. He wound the big ones and the small ones. He wound the cuckoo clock and the grandfather clock and the tinkly little Swiss clock.

Soon all the clocks began to talk.

TICKETY-TICK, TICKETY-TICK, whispered the little clocks.

TOCK-TOCK, said the big ones.

CUCKOO, CUCKOO, CUCKOO, whistled the cuckoo clock.

The grandfather clock chimed a cheery BONG-BONG, and the Swiss clock never stopped singing its tiny, tinkly song.

"Now, this is the way I *like* it," said Mr. Winky, holding a clock close to his ear. "I dearly love a cheerful shop, and who wants to hear himself think, anyhow?"